AF428999

This series was originally created and told by my mother, Ella Lang in the 1950's and I am honored to share her stories in this series of Pixie and Dixie to children everywhere. Always reach for the stars!



Book Author: Sharon (Gigi) Lang

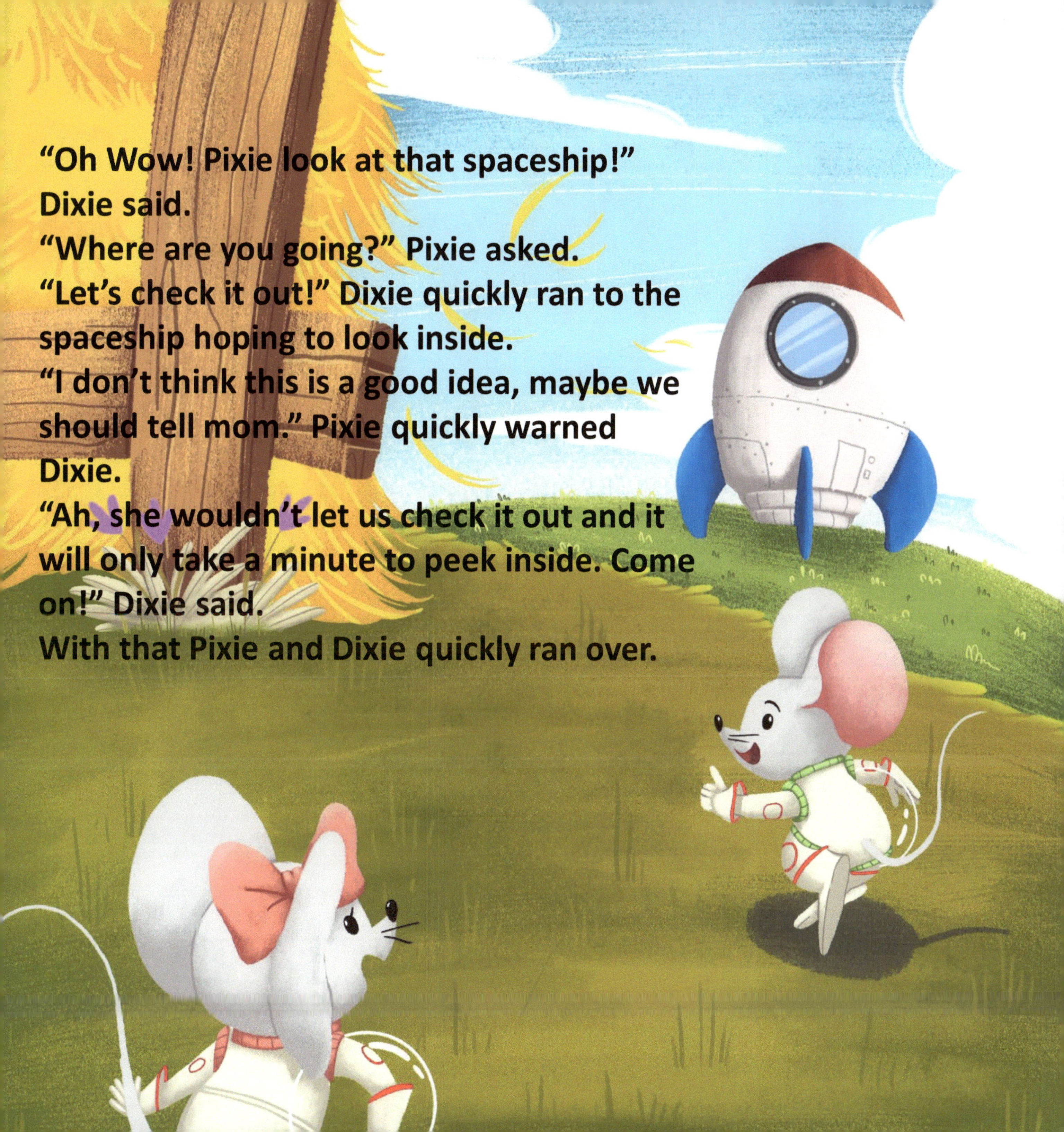

"Oh Wow! Pixie look at that spaceship!"
Dixie said.
"Where are you going?" Pixie asked.
"Let's check it out!" Dixie quickly ran to the
spaceship hoping to look inside.
"I don't think this is a good idea, maybe we
should tell mom." Pixie quickly warned
Dixie.
"Ah, she wouldn't let us check it out and it
will only take a minute to peek inside. Come
on!" Dixie said.
With that Pixie and Dixie quickly ran over.

"Look, there is a door over here, we can go in." Dixie quickly ran up the ramp.
"Wow, this sure is a tall spaceship." Pixie said walking up.

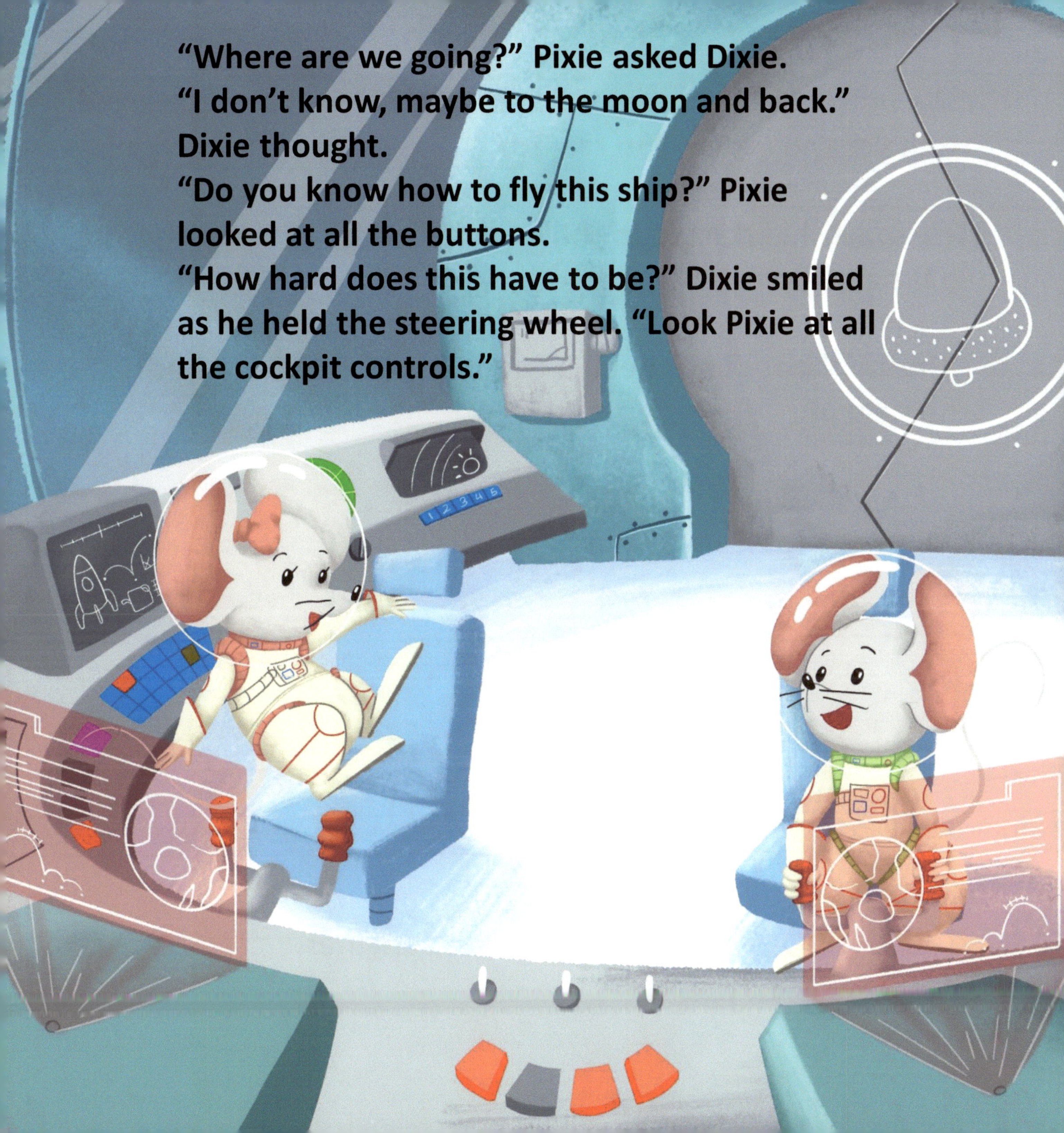

"Where are we going?" Pixie asked Dixie.
"I don't know, maybe to the moon and back." Dixie thought.
"Do you know how to fly this ship?" Pixie looked at all the buttons.
"How hard does this have to be?" Dixie smiled as he held the steering wheel. "Look Pixie at all the cockpit controls."

"We better get in our seats." Pixie replied as the ship started to shake and rattle. "I'm scared."

The spaceship started to shake and all of a sudden it started to lift and move upward into the clouds.

"This might not have been a good idea Dixie." Pixie said as she held on.

"Hold on!" Dixie yelled over the loud engines.

"Look Pixie, the stars are so bright." Dixie said gazing at the sight.

"There are so many!" Pixie said.  "Look at the asteroids!"

"Wow!  I wonder what those stars of made of?" Dixie asked.

"Stars are huge celestial bodies made mostly of hydrogen and helium that produce light and heat from the churning nuclear forges inside their cores." Pixie told Dixie.

Dixie just stared at Pixie and wondered how she knew.

"What is that big round cheese-like ball?" Dixie thought.

"I don't know, but I am getting hungry." Pixie replied.

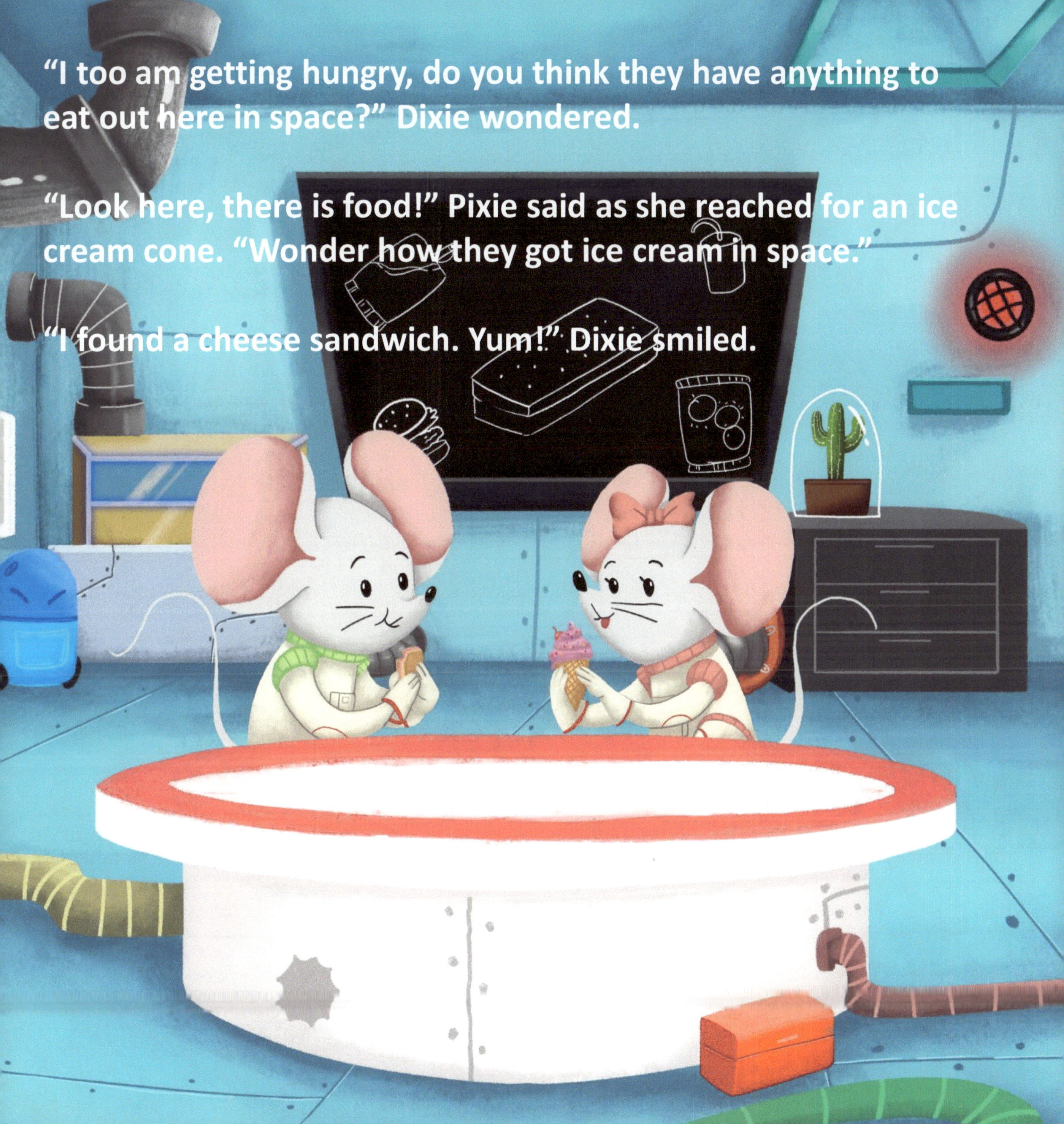

"I too am getting hungry, do you think they have anything to eat out here in space?" Dixie wondered.

"Look here, there is food!" Pixie said as she reached for an ice cream cone. "Wonder how they got ice cream in space."

"I found a cheese sandwich. Yum!" Dixie smiled.

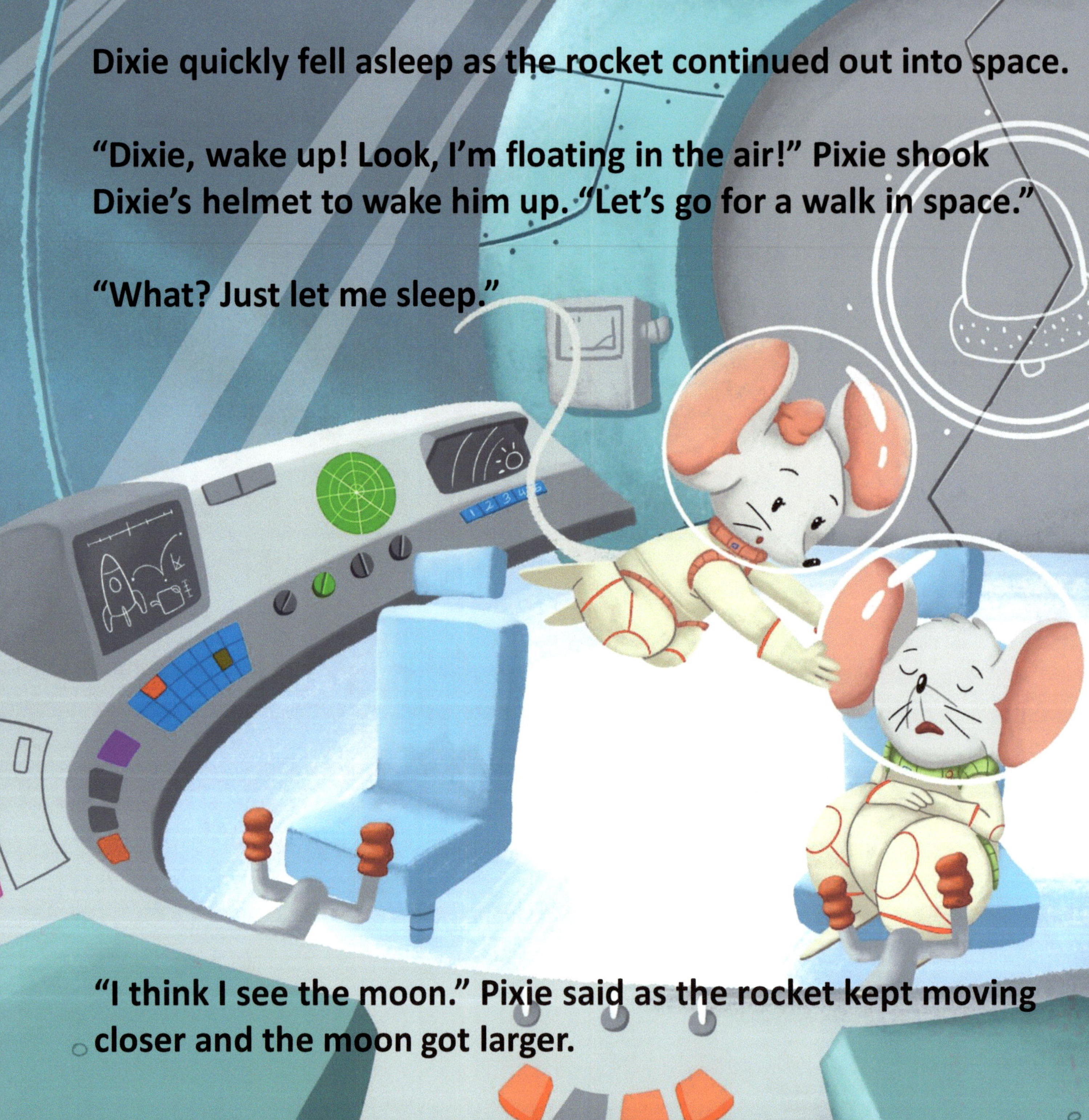

Dixie quickly fell asleep as the rocket continued out into space.

"Dixie, wake up! Look, I'm floating in the air!" Pixie shook Dixie's helmet to wake him up. "Let's go for a walk in space."

"What? Just let me sleep."

"I think I see the moon." Pixie said as the rocket kept moving closer and the moon got larger.

"Look over there, it is the moon!" Dixie pointed.

Pixie held on tight to the rocket as it moved amongst the stars.

"Nope, I'am not letting go!" Pixie said.

"Look, no hands!"

"Dixie, that isn't funny." Pixie replied.

"Look, there is Saturn with it's rings." Dixie said.

"Look.,a shooting star!  Hurry make a wish." Pixie said.

"I think I can touch the stars." Dixie held out his hands.

"It's the MOON!" They said at the same time.

Pixie and Dixie's spaceship raced toward the Moon.  Was it made of cheese, they wondered?

Pixie and Dixie landed on the moon. In the distance they could see Earth and the satellites orbiting the planet.

As the spaceship landed clouds of dust circled the ship.

"Hey look Pixie! We just landed on the Moon! There is no cheese, just dust." Dixie noted.

"Wow, this is amazing.  We are like Neil Armstrong!  Pixie said gleefully walking down the ramp.

"Look Pixie, I'm floating!
"Be careful!  You don't want to jump off the Moon and into space. There is no gravity to keep us down!"  Pixie warned Dixie.
"Wow, this is so cool!" Dixie continued to jump. "Look at Earth, it seems like I could reach out and touch it."
"The Moon is 238,900 miles away, you can't touch it!" Pixie laughed.

"Who put this here?" Dixie asked when he saw the US flag.

"Neil Armstrong and Buzz Aldrin in 1969." Pixie said. We should get back on the spaceship, it is getting late."

"We need to look for more food." Pixie told Dixie.

"I think we ate it all!" Dixie replied.

"Keep looking!" Pixie shouted as she looked around.

After digging through the drawers and cabinets,
they finally found a piece of … CHEESE!

"Pixie when we get home, I'm going to have the biggest meal EVER!" Dixie moaned. "We need to find more to eat, because I am still hungry."

"Me too." Pixie moaned back. "I'm still hungry and I miss Mom I want to go home."

It was time to pack up and leave.

"Dixie, close the hatch door."  Pixie told him as they prepared to leave.

"Got it!"

"We didn't plan this adventure very well. We are in such trouble for not telling her where we are going." Pixie told her brother.

"You're right Pixie, we should have gotten permission." Dixie noted.

"She's probably worried too."

"I want to go home!" Dixie cried out.

Just then...

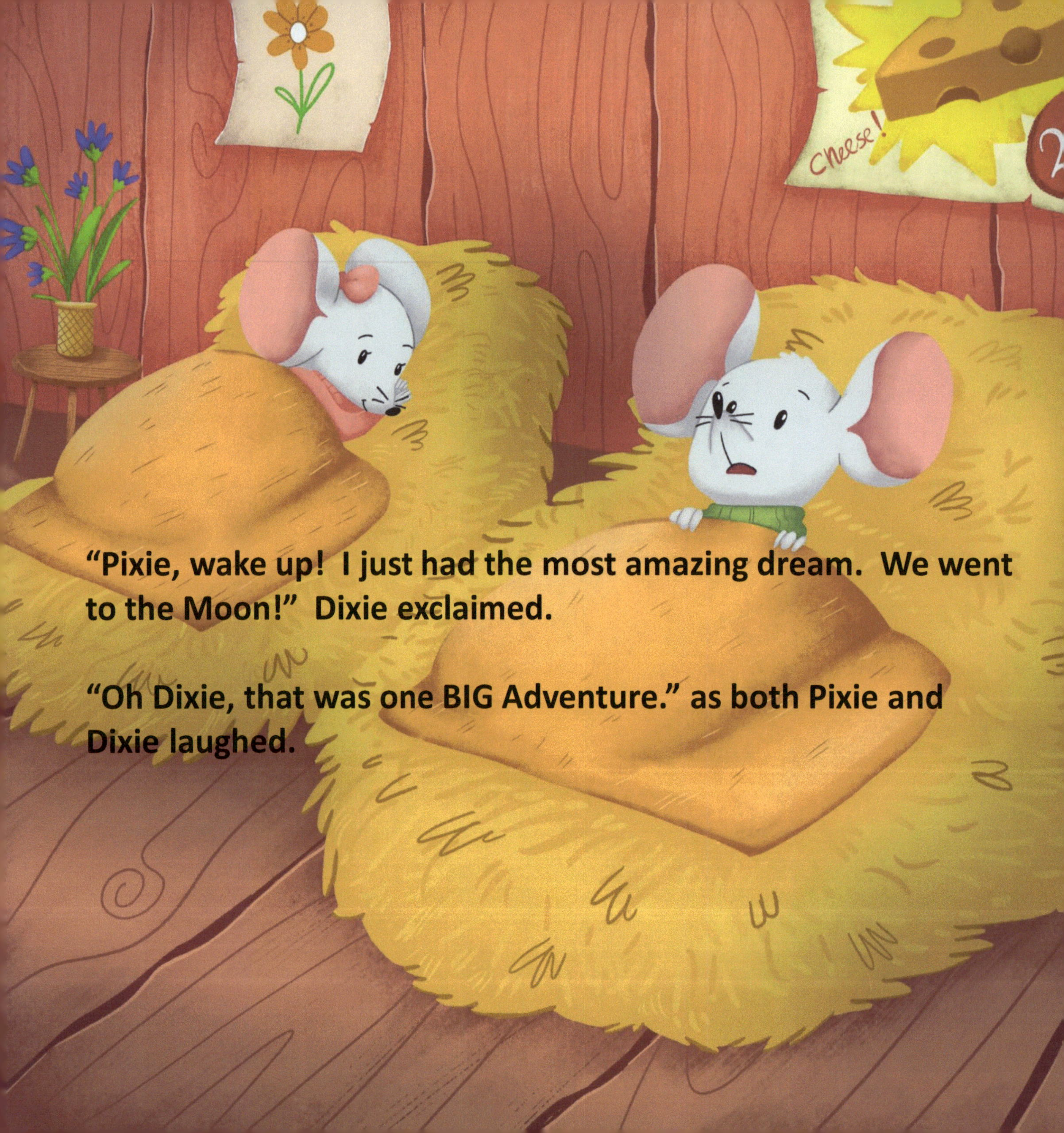

"Pixie, wake up!  I just had the most amazing dream.  We went to the Moon!"  Dixie exclaimed.

"Oh Dixie, that was one BIG Adventure." as both Pixie and Dixie laughed.

"Look at that Moon." Pixie noted.

"To think we went there in my adventurous dream." Dixie smiled.

"Good thing it was just a dream!" Pixie reminded him.

The Moon's :
<u>Distance to Earth</u>: 238,900 mi
<u>Orbital period</u>: 27 days
<u>Gravity</u>: 1.62 m/s²
<u>Radius</u>: 1,079.6 mi
<u>Age</u>: 4.53 billion years
<u>Orbits</u>: <u>Earth</u>
<u>Shape</u>: <u>Scalene ellipsoid</u>

Apollo 11 crew landed on the Moon on July 20, 1969.

How long would it take to drive to the Moon... it would take as long as driving around the world 10 times - just under six months.

How many elephants would it take to reach the Moon?
<u>Answer</u>: If you take the average height of an African elephant as 10 ft tall, then it would take 126,100,000 standing on each other's backs to reach the moon.

The average composition of the lunar surface by weight is roughly 43% oxygen, 20% silicon, 19% magnesium, 10% iron, 3% calcium, 3% aluminum, 0.42% chromium, 0.18% titanium and 0.12% manganese. Orbiting spacecraft have found traces of water on the lunar surface that may have originated from deep underground.

Armstrong and Aldrin had trouble inserting the pole into the lunar surface, and only managed to get it about seven inches deep. When they backed away from the flag, it proved it could stand on its own. Scientists discovered later that the lunar dust has a different profile than terrestrial dust.

## SPACE FOOD FACTS

Imagine going camping for more than a week with several of your close friends. You would make sure you have plenty of food and the gear to cook and eat it with.

Astronauts basically do the same thing when they go to space. There are no refrigerators in space, so space food must be stored and prepared properly to avoid spoilage, especially on longer missions.

Condiments, such as ketchup, mustard and mayonnaise, are provided. Salt and pepper are available but only in a liquid form. This is because astronauts can't sprinkle salt and pepper on their food in space. The salt and pepper would simply float away. There is a danger they could clog air vents, contaminate equipment or get stuck in an astronaut's eyes, mouth or nose.

As on Earth, space food comes in disposable packages. Some packaging actually prevents food from flying away. The food packaging is designed to be flexible and easier to use, as well as to maximize space when stowing or disposing of food containers.

Learn more at nasa.gov

Other books by Gigi Lang for Children
Pixie & Dixie
Pumpkin Adventure
By Gigi Lang
The Adventures of
PIXIE AND DIXIE
Go To Market
By Gigi Lang
What's A Pandemic Mommy?
BY : GIGI LANG
SECOND EDITION
I am
I am, a lion
I AM!
Written by - Gigi Lang
Additional Adventures of Pixie and Dixie coming soon.